GARFIELD Sumo Beach Bellyball

Created by
JIM DAVIS

Written by Jugnoo Husain
Designed and illustrated by Mike Fentz

This edition published in 2002 by Troll Communications L.L.C.
All rights reserved. No part of this book may be reproduced or utilized in any form or by
any means, electronic or mechanical, including photocopying, recording, or by any
information storage and retrieval system, without written permission from the publisher.
ISBN 0-8167-7430-7   Printed in the United States of America.
10 9 8 7 6 5 4 3 2 1

MW01056526

Jon, **Garfield, and Odie** had just arrived at their hotel for a month-long vacation in California. Jon had already changed into his sandals and polka-dot swimming trunks.

"What, no matching socks?" cracked Garfield.

"Surfing, anyone?" asked Jon, putting on his rubber-ducky inner tube.

"I only surf TV channels," thought Garfield, lovingly patting the remote control. Odie just drooled. When Jon didn't get any response, he decided to go to the beach alone.

Suddenly a television commercial caught Garfield's attention.

"Odie," he yelled. "Stop chasing your tail and listen to this!"

"Want unlimited free food?" the announcer bellowed. "Not worried about gaining weight? Well, come on down to the TV station and sign up for the extremely radical Sumo Beach Bellyball Contest!"

"Too cool!" exclaimed Garfield. "California is still the land of opportunity!"

The announcer explained that two sumo wrestlers on a promotional tour were challenging any daring duo to a game of "beach bellyball."

"It's just like beach volleyball, except you can't use your hands or arms," the announcer continued. "All other body parts are fair game, especially your belly. Challengers must be in the same weight class as the sumo champions. So area restaurants are donating free food to help fatten up the lucky contenders. And if you beat the champs, you'll win a year's supply of free pizza!"

"Say no more," said Garfield as he dragged a confused Odie out the door. "I'm already close to sumo size. But if you're going to be my partner, Odie, you've got to bulk up."

"Huh?" said Odie.

"Never mind," said Garfield. "Just follow me and we'll GROW places!"

Being selected for the contest was easy—no one else wanted to gain so much weight. So Garfield and Odie put their paw prints on the contract and headed out to eat.

They were treated like royalty in every restaurant. Garfield slurped and burped, urging Odie to pig out, too.

"No guts, no glory," said Garfield, patting his bulging belly. "So scarf till you barf!"

Finally the restaurants ran out of food, and Garfield and Odie belched and waddled their way back to the hotel. The fat cat was already gleefully anticipating the next day's dishes.

"I am not happy about this," said Jon when he learned what his pets had done.

But by now Garfield and Odie were famous. Their story was already on the evening news. Jon reluctantly agreed to let them compete.

"You'll both have to go on strict diets when this is over," he warned.

"Fat chance," quipped Garfield, thinking only about the year's supply of pizza if his team won.

So the routine was set. Garfield and Odie had three weeks to *round* into shape. They trained hard—day and night, night and day, eating and sleeping, sleeping and eating, till at last they were so fat, Jon had to feed them with a shovel!

For bellyball practice, they tried to toss marshmallows back and forth with their jelly bellies. Of course, practice never lasted long because Garfield kept eating the marshmallows.

Finally the day of the big contest arrived. Dressed in psychedelic loincloths, the potbellied pets put on funky wraparound sunglasses.

"I'm so cool I'm jealous of myself," crowed Garfield, as he admired his bodacious bod in the mirror. Odie, who now looked more like a hog than a dog, merely oinked.

A large crowd had gathered on the beach. Garfield and Odie approached their opponents, whose HUGE bodies glistened with oil. The sumo wrestlers bowed politely.

"I'm Lardo and this is Porko," the captain said. Garfield and Odie tried to bow, but Odie, who wasn't used to being so fat, toppled over.

"I'm Garfield and this is Odie," said Garfield. "But you can call us Jumbo and Dumbo."

Lardo's team won the coin toss to serve first.

"We'll play to 15 points, 'rally scoring' method," explained the referee. "That means you don't have to serve to score; every time the ball hits the ground a point is awarded. Okay, boys, let the game begin!"

FOMP!

With that, Lardo smacked the ball across the net with his massive gut. Odie tried to use his head to set the ball up for Garfield, but the portly pooch was now way too slow, and the ball plopped on the sand.

The next serve came toward Garfield, who wiggled and jiggled his tummy and "bellybopped" the ball over the net.
"Take that, Sumo Breath," taunted Garfield.

But his joy was short-lived. Porko easily "gutted" the ball back over the net toward the bumbling, stumbling Odie. Lardo and Porko won the point, then many, many more in rapid succession. The sumos were playing like the champions they were. They were pros; Garfield and Odie were just fatsos.

The pets found themselves on the brink of defeat, 14–0, when a desperate Garfield called time out. He and Odie huddled.

"Listen, Drool Bucket," instructed Garfield. "Instead of tripping over your tongue, why don't you use it to whack that ball?!"

For once Odie seemed to understand. He nodded excitedly. And so the game resumed.

SMACK! THWACK! Odie's killer tongue was everywhere, walloping the ball like a tennis racquet. Garfield's plan was working! Incredibly enough, the score was soon tied. The pets were now only one point away from victory.

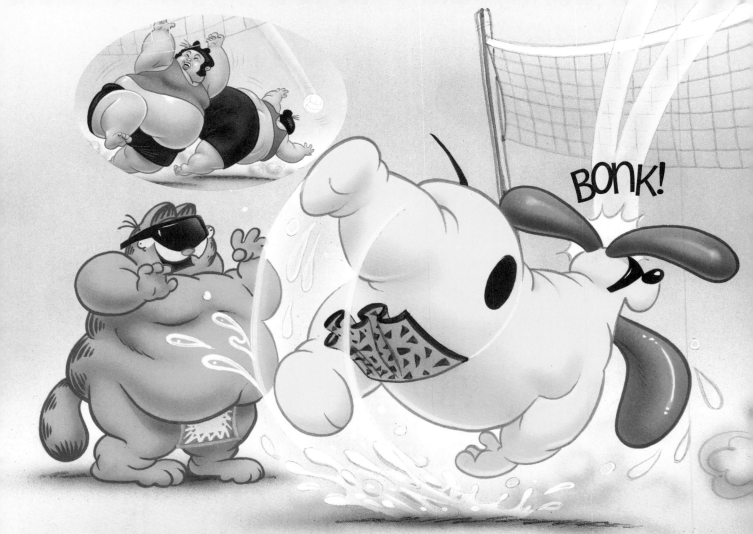

The final volley came toward Odie. He tried to spike it with his mighty tongue, but he had drooled so much that he slipped on his own saliva. The ball bounced off his head instead and amazingly rocketed over the net, landing just beyond the reach of Lardo and Porko.

"We won! We actually won!" shouted Garfield, already dreaming of his pizzas. "Odie, that empty skull of yours acted like a springboard for that ball!"

"Wow, that was some head shot!" exclaimed Porko, as he and Lardo stepped forward to congratulate the winners.

"Odie may be brainless," said Garfield, grinning, "but for once in his life, he actually used his head!"